This book
was presented
to

_____

by

_____

on

_____

Heaven on Earth

Illustrations © Copyright 2006 Dona Gelsinger,
Little Angel Publishing, Inc., White City, OR. All rights reserved.
The LIL' ANGELS name and logo are trademarks of
Dona Gelsinger, Little Angel Publishing, Inc.
Text Copyright © 2006 Dalmatian Press, LLC
Published in 2006 by Spirit Press, an imprint of Dalmatian Press, LLC.

Illustrator: *Dona Gelsinger*
Writer: *Peggy Shaw*
Designer: *Marva J. Martin*

The SPIRIT PRESS and DALMATIAN PRESS names and logos
are trademarks of Dalmatian Press, LLC, Franklin, Tennessee 37067.
No part of this book may be reproduced or copied in any form
without the written permission of Dalmatian Press.

ISBN: 1-40373-260-4
15969/0906

Printed in the U.S.A.

06 07 08 09 LBM 10 9 8 7 6 5 4 3 2 1

Heaven on Earth

Heaven on Earth

Illustrated by Dona Gelsinger

Written by Peggy Shaw

SPIRIT PRESS

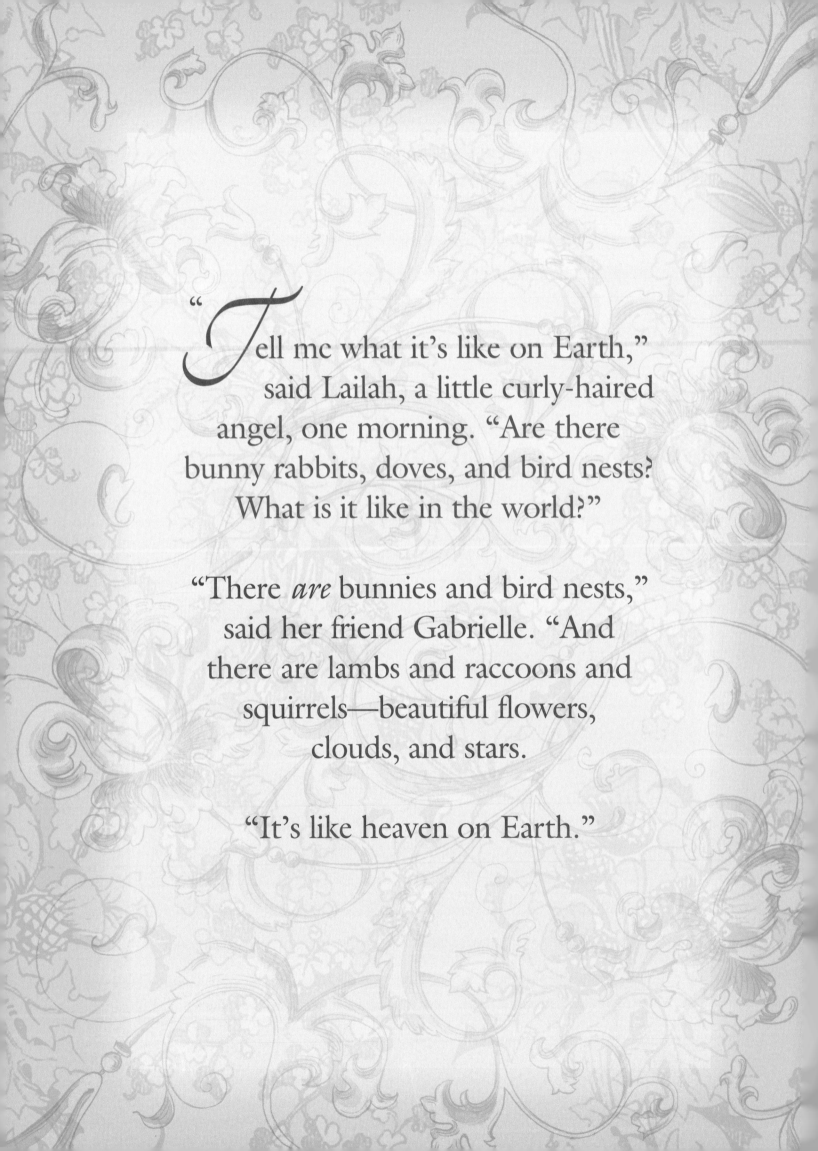

"Tell me what it's like on Earth," said Lailah, a little curly-haired angel, one morning. "Are there bunny rabbits, doves, and bird nests? What is it like in the world?"

"There *are* bunnies and bird nests," said her friend Gabrielle. "And there are lambs and raccoons and squirrels—beautiful flowers, clouds, and stars.

"It's like heaven on Earth."

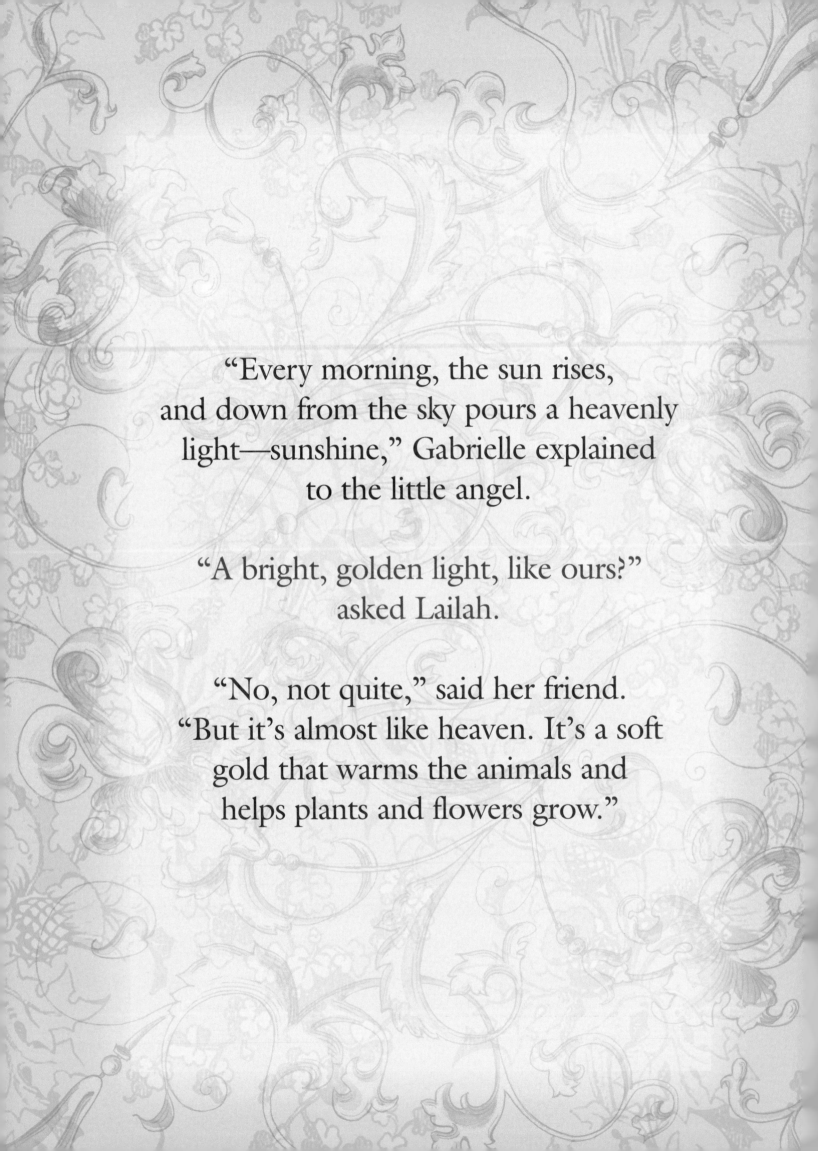

"Every morning, the sun rises, and down from the sky pours a heavenly light—sunshine," Gabrielle explained to the little angel.

"A bright, golden light, like ours?" asked Lailah.

"No, not quite," said her friend. "But it's almost like heaven. It's a soft gold that warms the animals and helps plants and flowers grow."

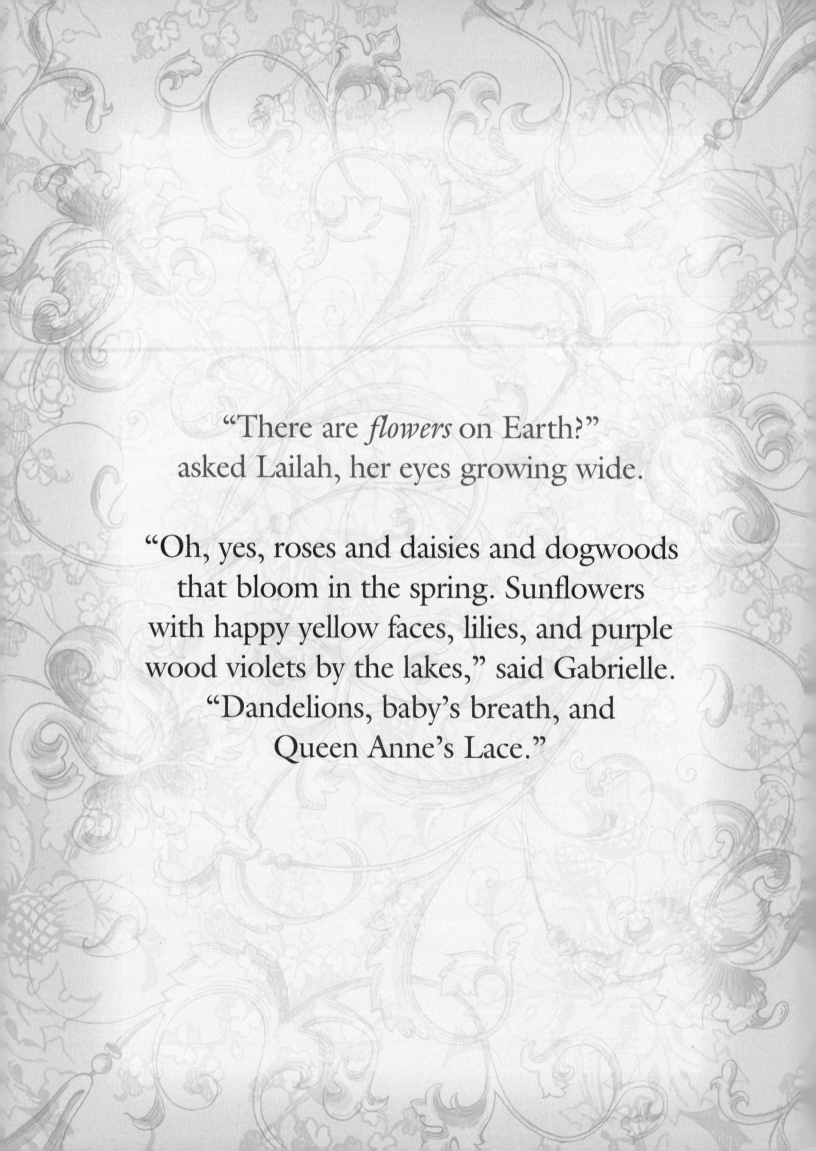

"There are *flowers* on Earth?"
asked Lailah, her eyes growing wide.

"Oh, yes, roses and daisies and dogwoods
that bloom in the spring. Sunflowers
with happy yellow faces, lilies, and purple
wood violets by the lakes," said Gabrielle.
"Dandelions, baby's breath, and
Queen Anne's Lace."

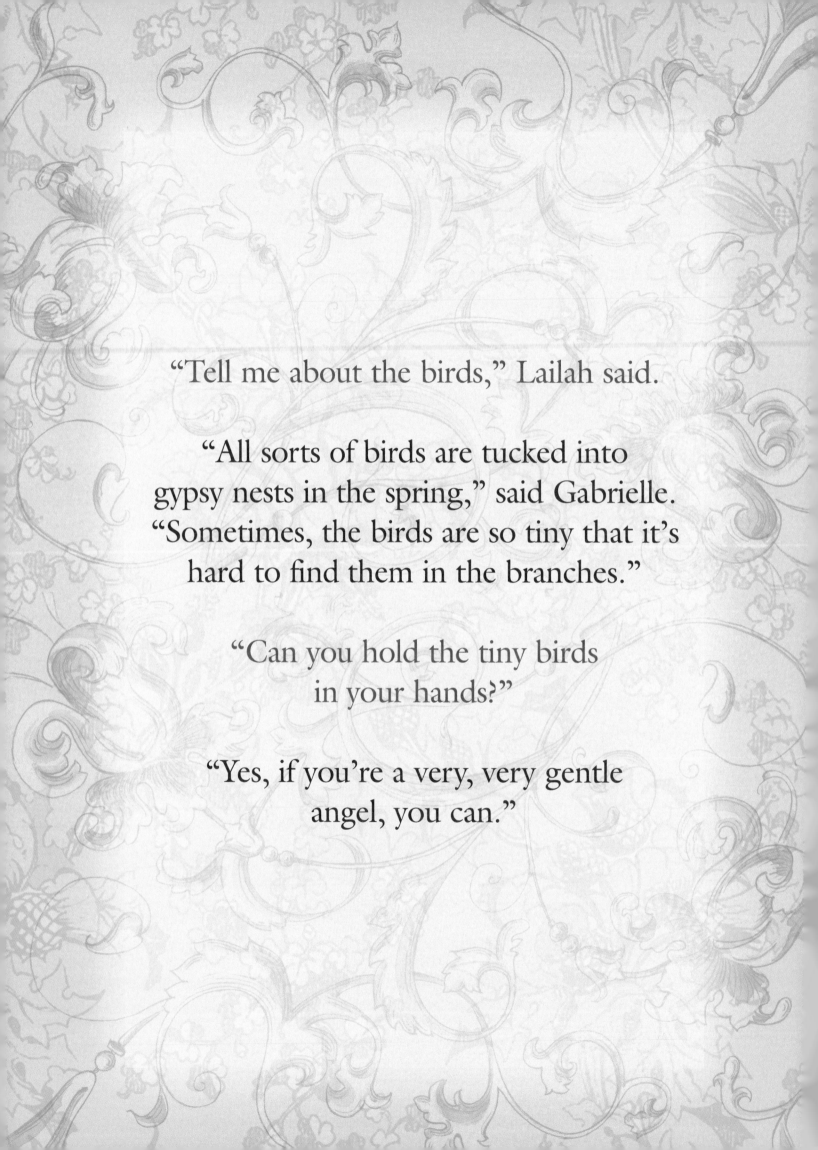

"Tell me about the birds," Lailah said.

"All sorts of birds are tucked into gypsy nests in the spring," said Gabrielle. "Sometimes, the birds are so tiny that it's hard to find them in the branches."

"Can you hold the tiny birds in your hands?"

"Yes, if you're a very, very gentle angel, you can."

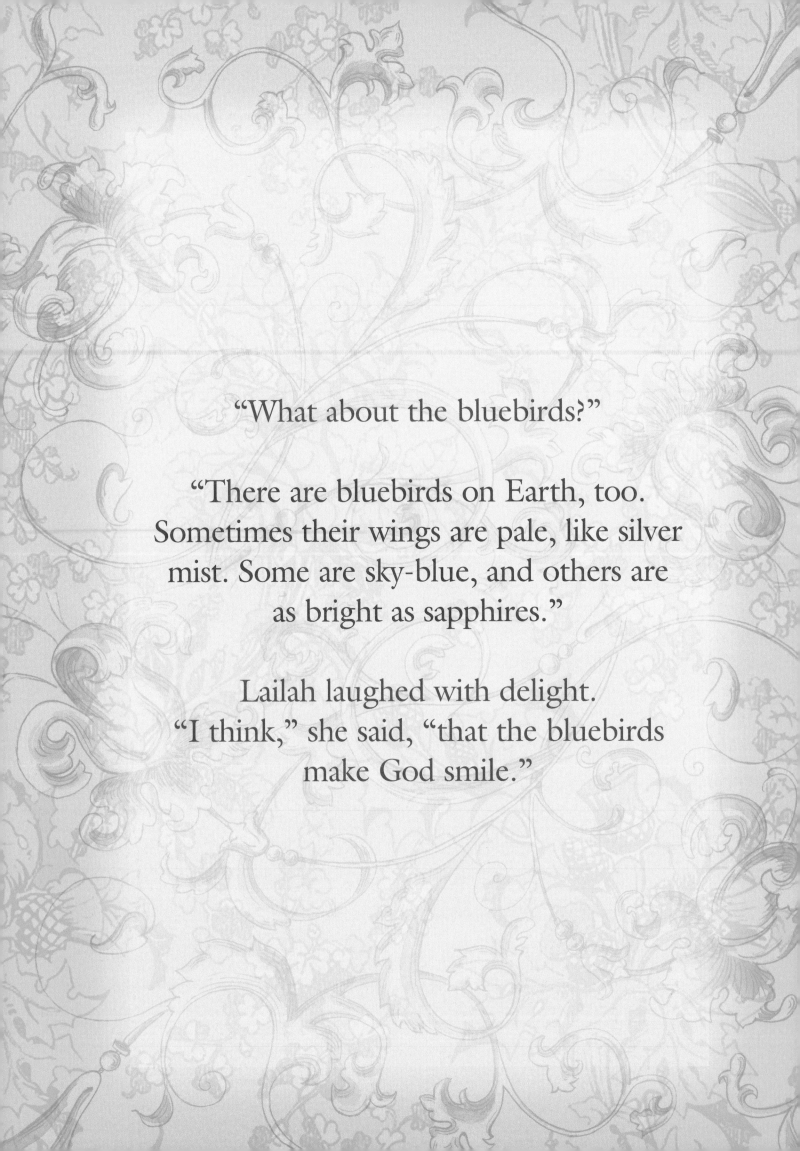

"What about the bluebirds?"

"There are bluebirds on Earth, too.
Sometimes their wings are pale, like silver
mist. Some are sky-blue, and others are
as bright as sapphires."

Lailah laughed with delight.
"I think," she said, "that the bluebirds
make God smile."

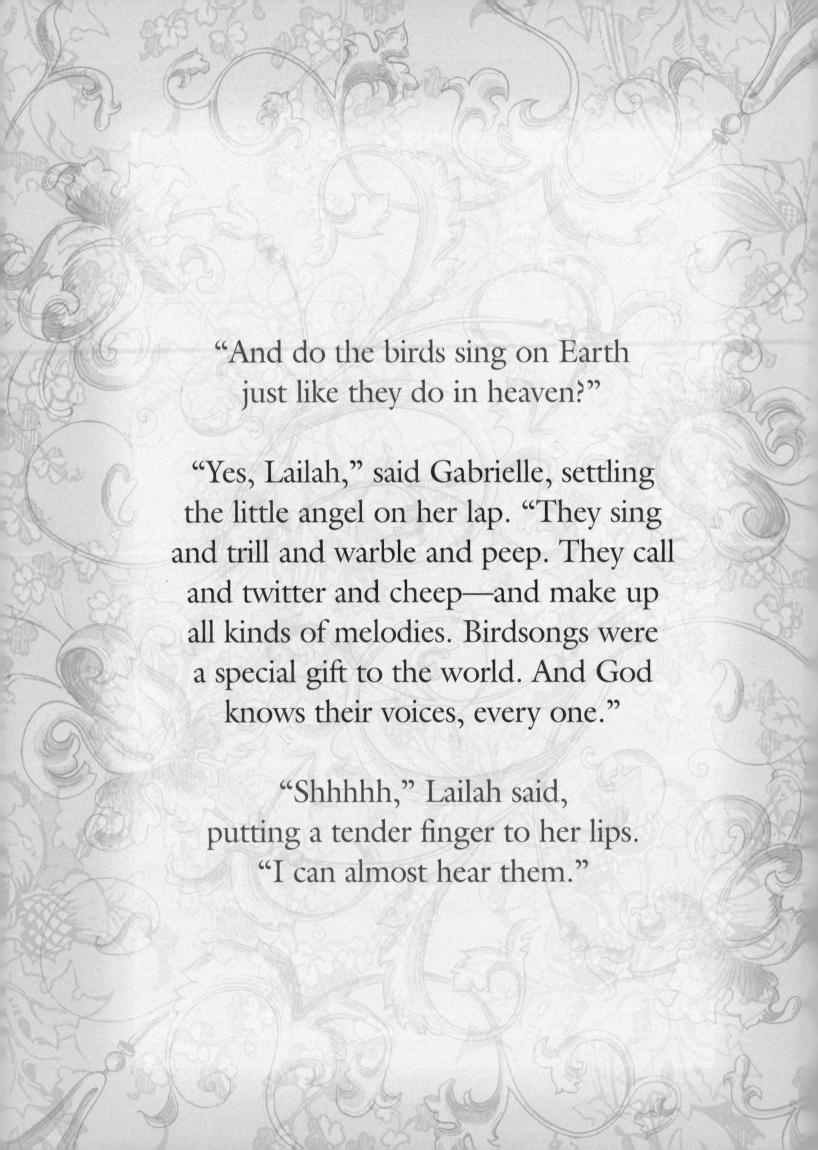

"And do the birds sing on Earth
just like they do in heaven?"

"Yes, Lailah," said Gabrielle, settling
the little angel on her lap. "They sing
and trill and warble and peep. They call
and twitter and cheep—and make up
all kinds of melodies. Birdsongs were
a special gift to the world. And God
knows their voices, every one."

"Shhhhh," Lailah said,
putting a tender finger to her lips.
"I can almost hear them."

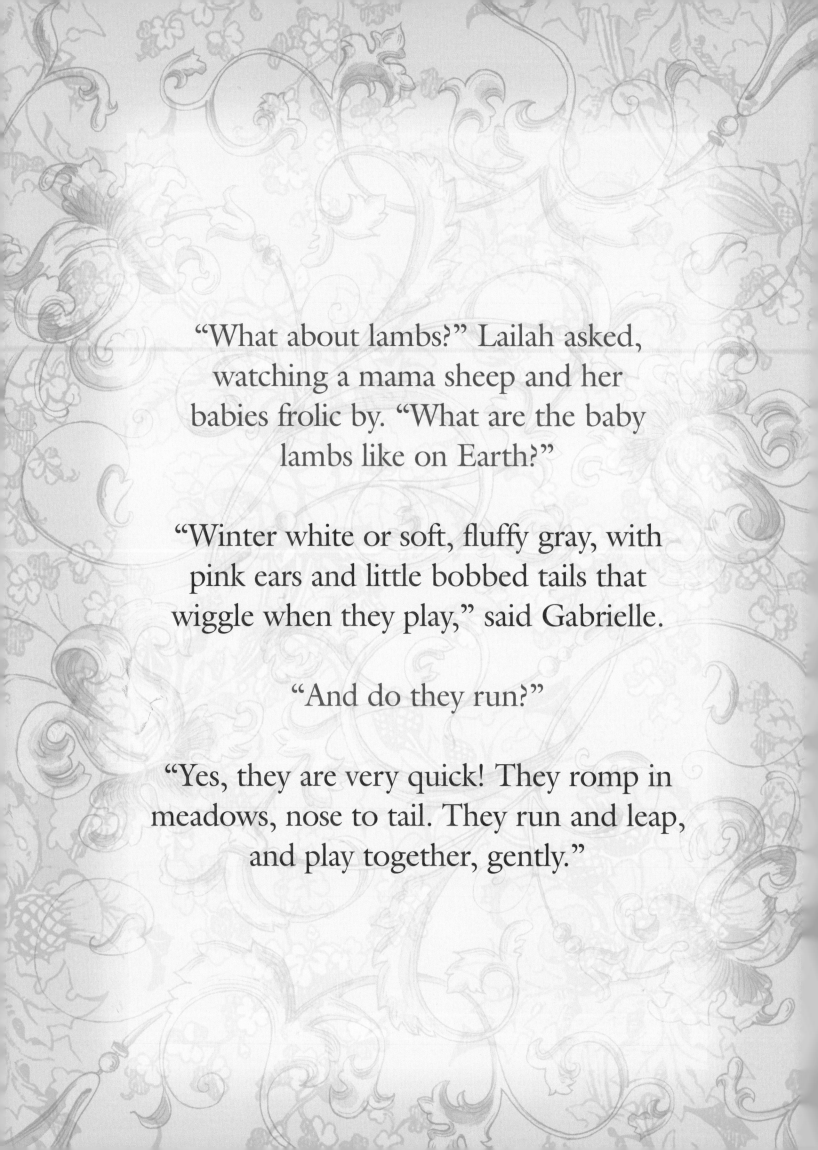

"What about lambs?" Lailah asked, watching a mama sheep and her babies frolic by. "What are the baby lambs like on Earth?"

"Winter white or soft, fluffy gray, with pink ears and little bobbed tails that wiggle when they play," said Gabrielle.

"And do they run?"

"Yes, they are very quick! They romp in meadows, nose to tail. They run and leap, and play together, gently."

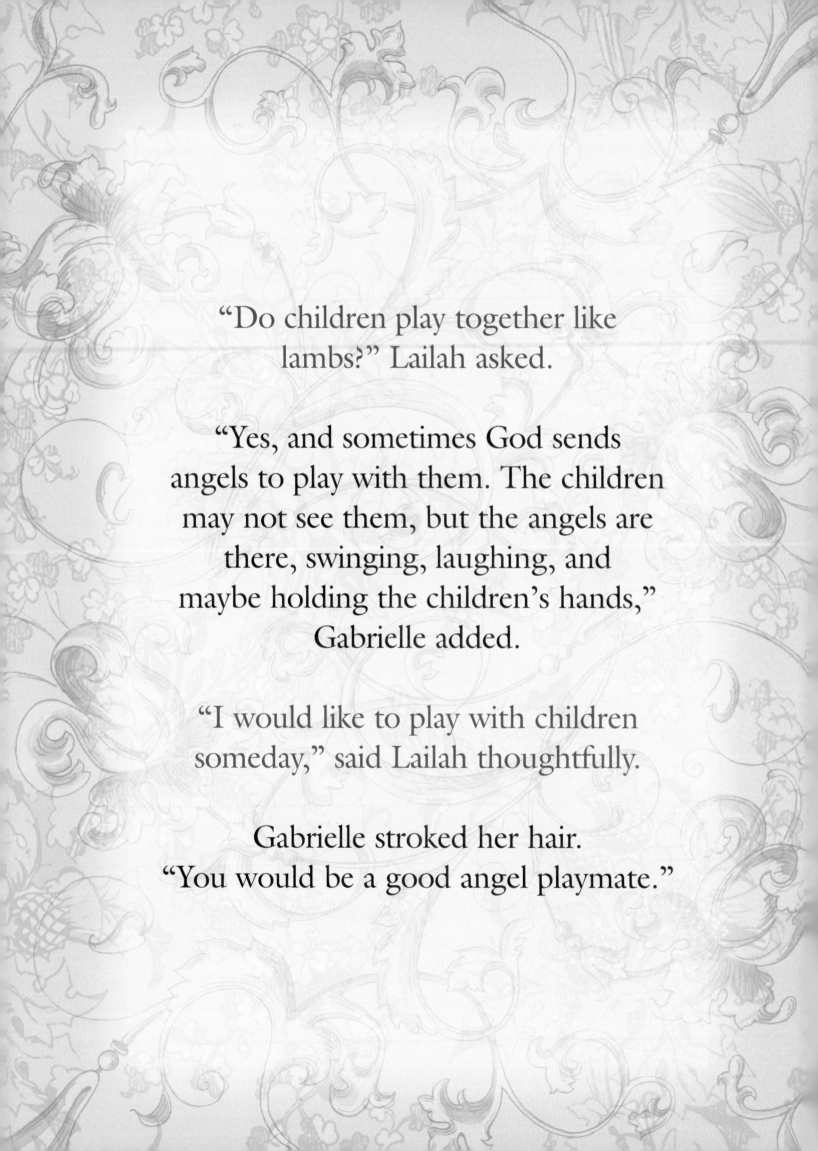

"Do children play together like lambs?" Lailah asked.

"Yes, and sometimes God sends angels to play with them. The children may not see them, but the angels are there, swinging, laughing, and maybe holding the children's hands," Gabrielle added.

"I would like to play with children someday," said Lailah thoughtfully.

Gabrielle stroked her hair.
"You would be a good angel playmate."

"Is it always spring where the children play on Earth?" wondered Lailah.

"No, after spring comes summer," Gabrielle said. "And some children go to the seashore."

"What is the seashore?"

"A place with shining water, like a brilliant sky that ripples in waves. There is sand—millions of fine, loose grains to walk in—and treasures called seashells that the waves bring in."

Lailah daydreamed about the seashore. "How do you know?" she said softly.

"Because I was there, a long time ago."

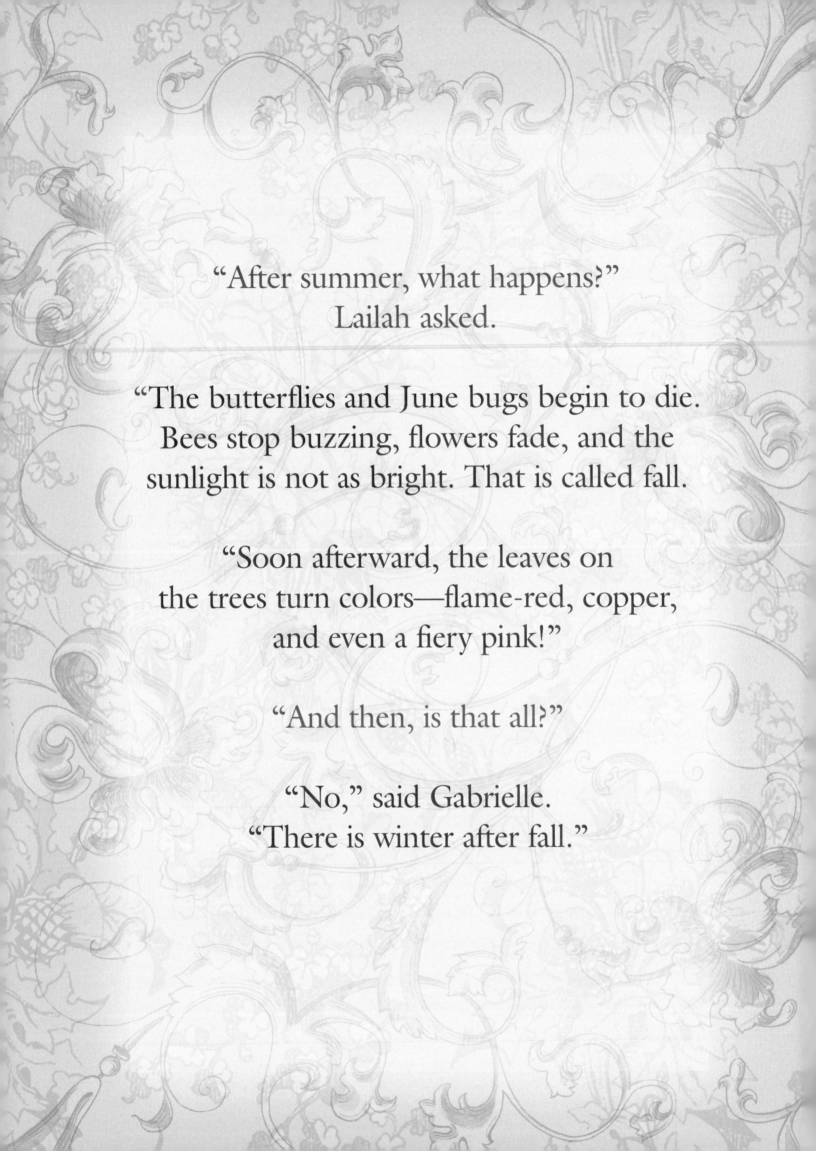

"After summer, what happens?"
Lailah asked.

"The butterflies and June bugs begin to die.
Bees stop buzzing, flowers fade, and the
sunlight is not as bright. That is called fall.

"Soon afterward, the leaves on
the trees turn colors—flame-red, copper,
and even a fiery pink!"

"And then, is that all?"

"No," said Gabrielle.
"There is winter after fall."

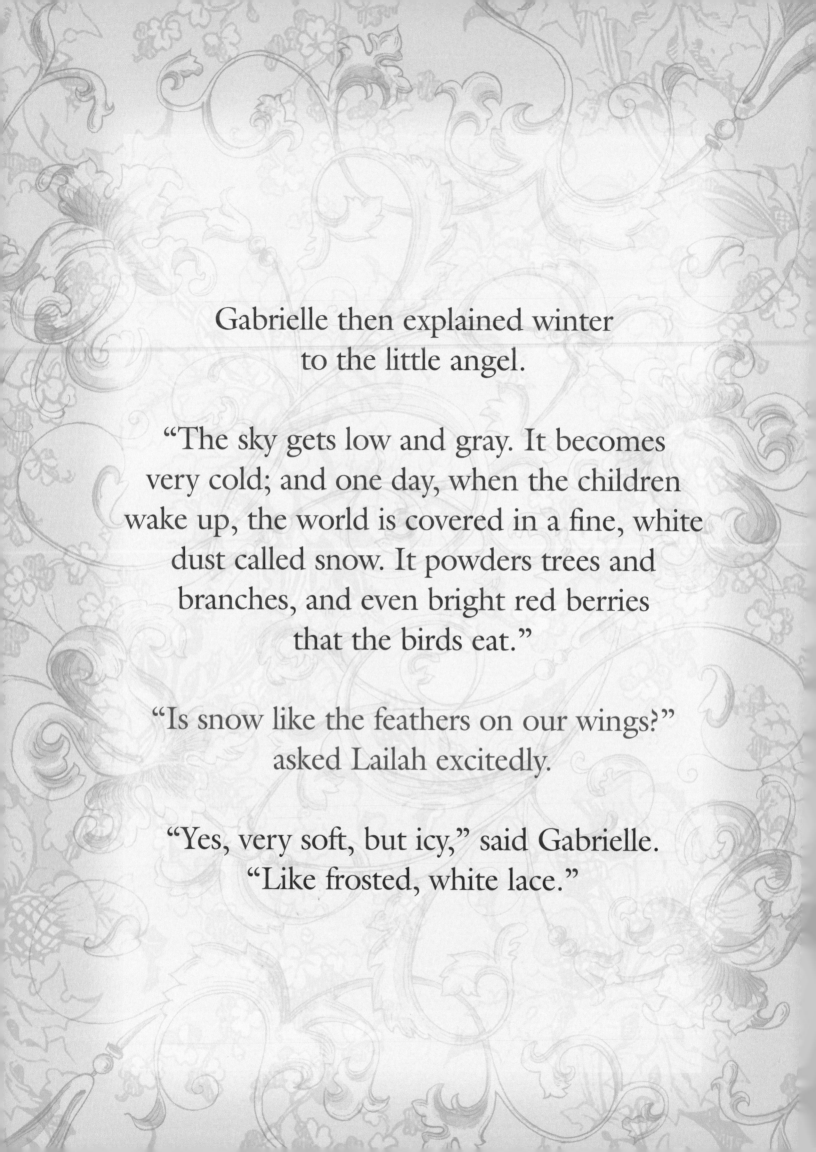

Gabrielle then explained winter
to the little angel.

"The sky gets low and gray. It becomes
very cold; and one day, when the children
wake up, the world is covered in a fine, white
dust called snow. It powders trees and
branches, and even bright red berries
that the birds eat."

"Is snow like the feathers on our wings?"
asked Lailah excitedly.

"Yes, very soft, but icy," said Gabrielle.
"Like frosted, white lace."

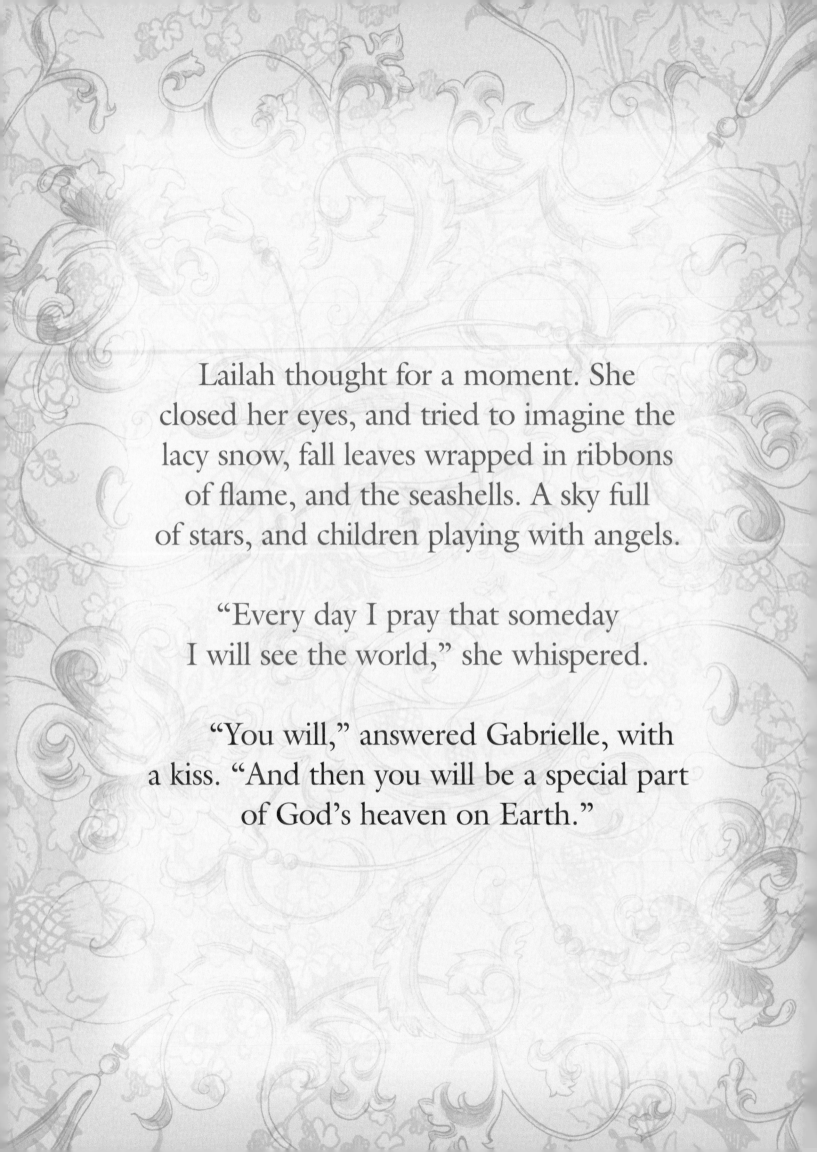

Lailah thought for a moment. She
closed her eyes, and tried to imagine the
lacy snow, fall leaves wrapped in ribbons
of flame, and the seashells. A sky full
of stars, and children playing with angels.

"Every day I pray that someday
I will see the world," she whispered.

"You will," answered Gabrielle, with
a kiss. "And then you will be a special part
of God's heaven on Earth."

For Lovely Things

We thank You, dear God,
For all lovely things:

For the pretty flowers
And the little birds
that sing;
For the butterflies,
The green grass,
and the trees;

We thank You,
dear God,
For all these
lovely things.

Edna Dean Baker

For lovely things I hear and see,

And happy thoughts that come to me;

Thank You, God,

our Father

Elizabeth McE. Shields

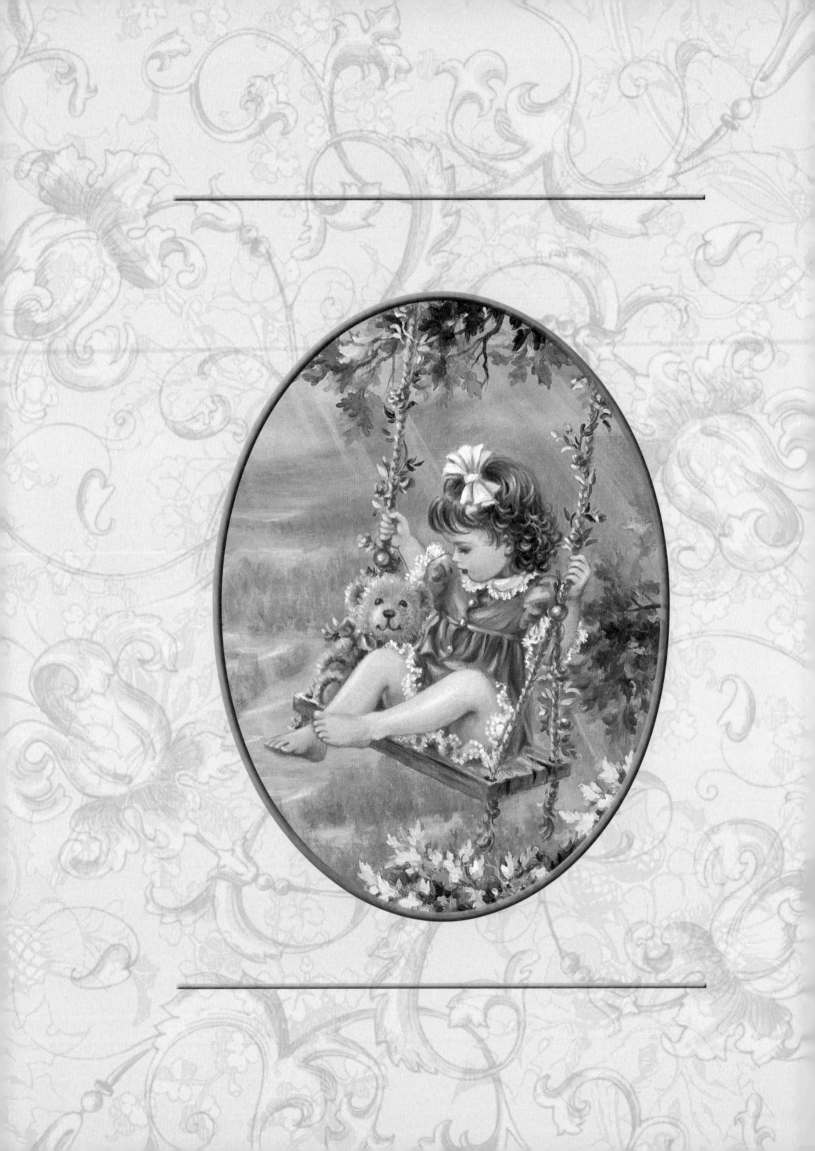

seesaw

jump rope

merry-go-round

Sports

basketball

snowshoes

sled

scooter

skis

bat and ball

hockey
puck

soccer ball

ice skates

football

9

Party

whistle

present

ice cream

photograph

camera

strawberries

juice

plate

cake

candle

party hat

spoon fork

11

Classroom

cassette player

globe

cassette

scissors

ruler

crayons

paintbrush

chalk

eraser

books

clock

computer

13

Doctor's Office

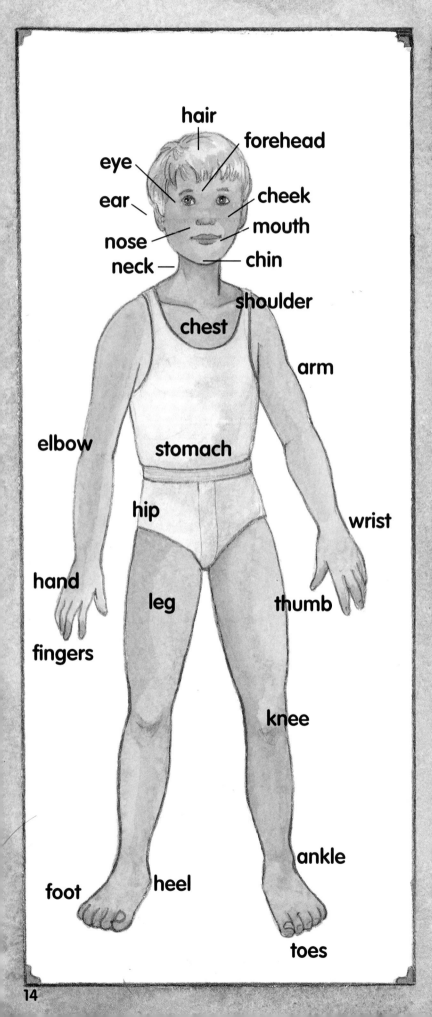

hair
forehead
eye
ear
cheek
mouth
nose
chin
neck
shoulder
chest
arm
elbow
stomach
hip
wrist
hand
leg
thumb
fingers
knee
ankle
foot
heel
toes

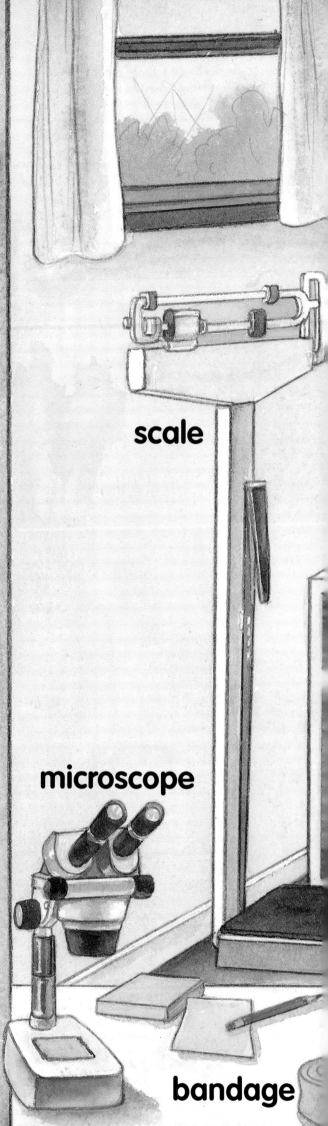

scale

microscope

bandage

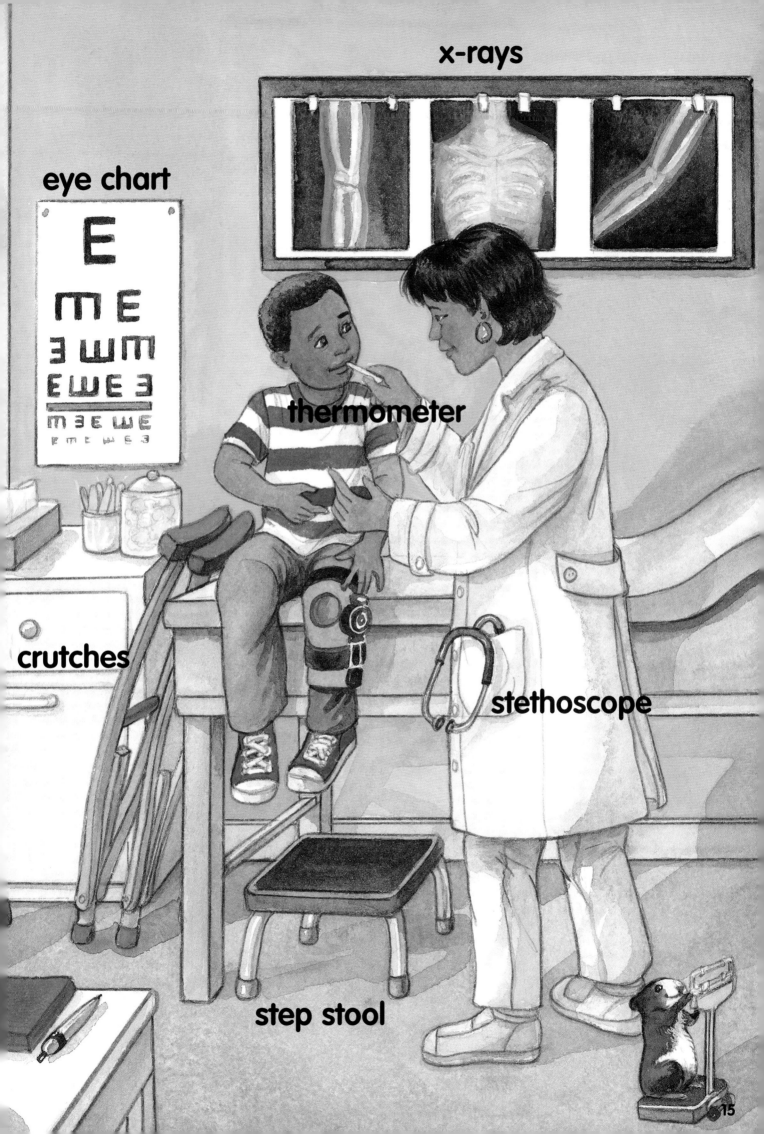

eye chart

x-rays

thermometer

crutches

stethoscope

step stool

15

watermelon

corn

sheep

bee

Farm

haystack

chicken

rooster

apples

pears

Grocery Store

cupcake

eggs

orange

tomato

carrots

bread

cheese

juice

lettuce

dog food

lemons

fish

Construction Site

crane

excavator

dump truck

welding torch

bulldozer

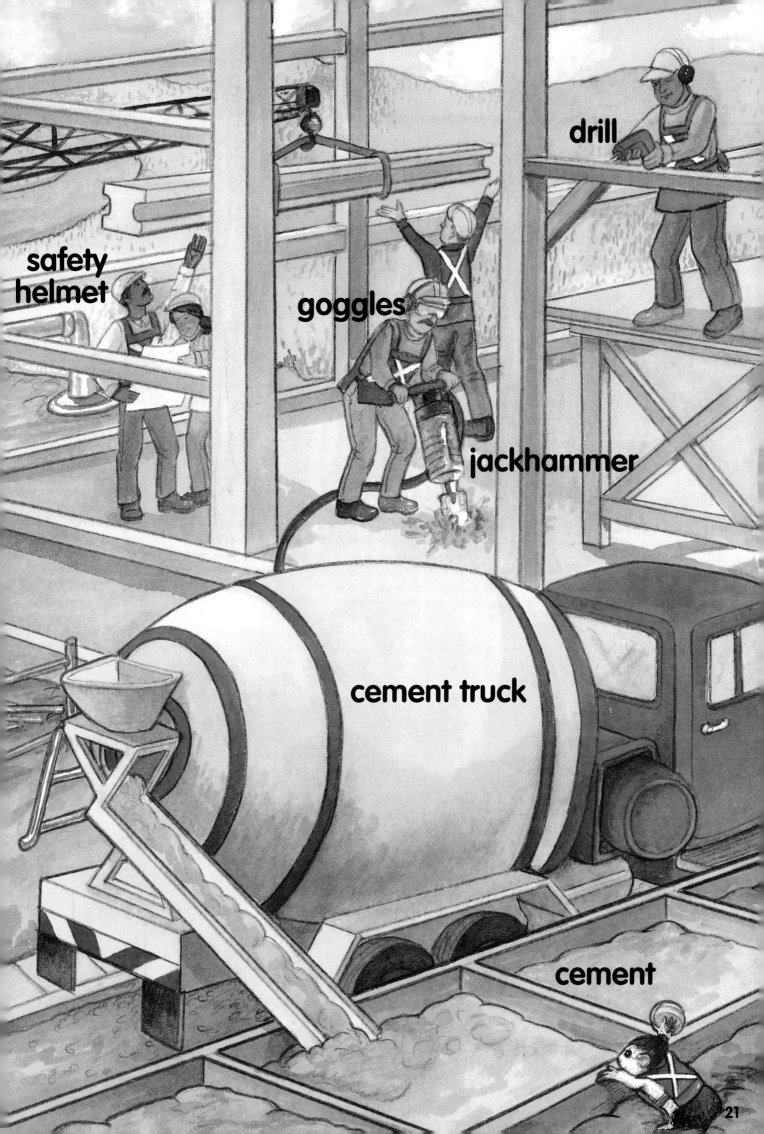

safety
helmet

goggles

drill

jackhammer

cement truck

cement

21

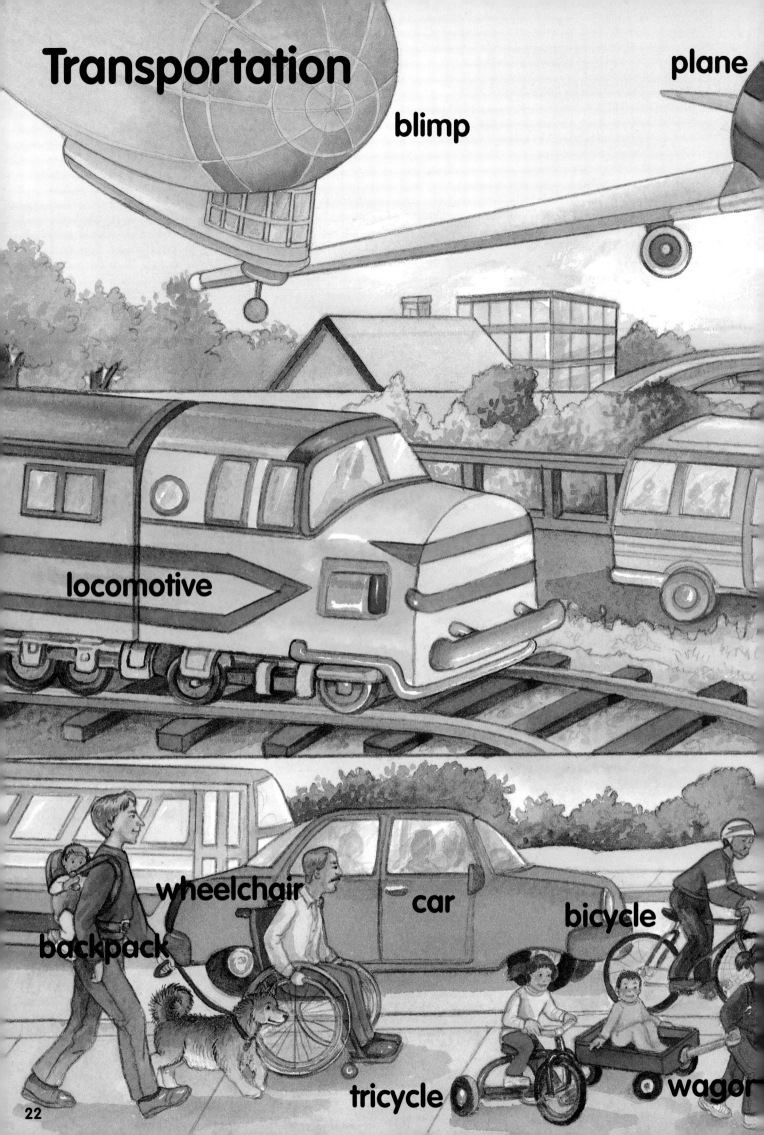

Transportation

plane

blimp

locomotive

wheelchair

car

bicycle

backpack

tricycle

wagon

22

helicopter

train

bus

motorcycle

van

taxi

scooter

Wild Animals

eagle

mountain goat

elk

beaver

bear

mountain lion

wolf

mountains

coyote

armadillo

roadrunner

owl

rattlesnake

tarantula

horned toad

desert

24

falcon

bison

mustang

meadowlark

jackrabbit

prairie dog

prairie

egret

ibis

deer

heron

manatee

flamingo

alligator

swamp

25

Pets

hardest

smallest

prickliest

hairiest

longest

softest

turtle

kittens

cat

fish

mouse snake

iguana

puppy

amsters hedgehogs parrot

rabbit

cockatoo

dog

lamp

pants

pajamas

shoes

socks

shorts

Bedroom

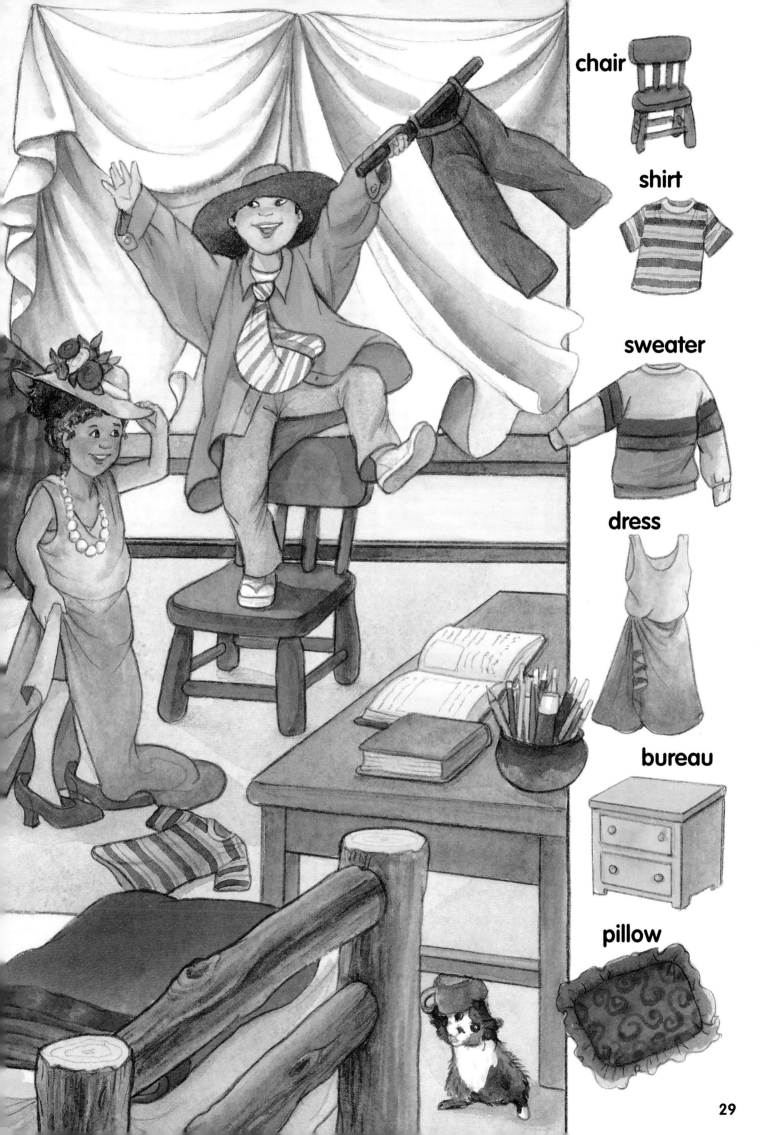

chair

shirt

sweater

dress

bureau

pillow

29

Bathroom

robe

underpants

towel

toothpaste

toothbrush

rubber duck

soap

Family Room

curtains

vase

television

rug

plant

lamp

portraits

chair

books

couch

offee table

33

Kitchen

pot

step stool

apron

frying pan

soap

tea kettle

cup

knife

sponge

timer

35

Garden

birdbath

rake

pumpkin

flowers

peas

carrots

wheelbarrow

36

flowerpot

Games and Toys

doll house

marionette

marbles

doll

truck

top

train

ball

cards

computer games

coloring book

puzzle

crayons

joystick

board game

checkers

blocks

38

Beach

sailboat

seashell

pail

rowboat

shovel

kayak

seagull

umbrella

swimsuit

sand castle

beach towel

Ocean

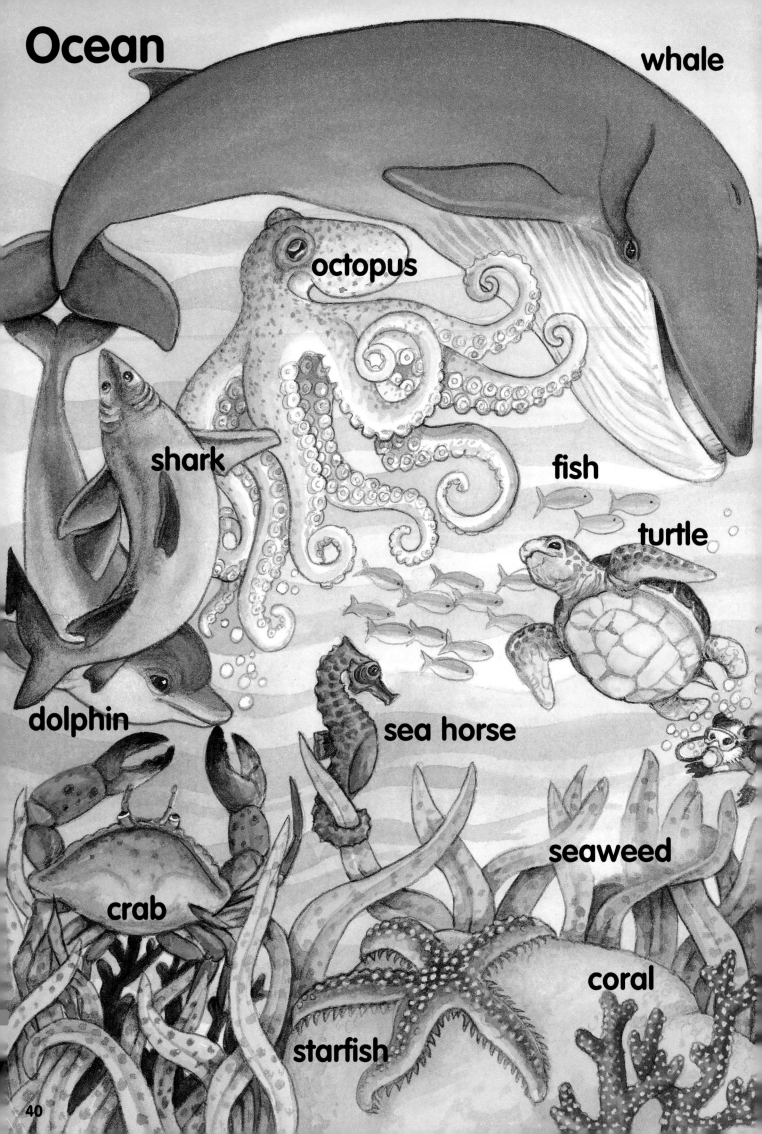

whale

octopus

shark

fish

turtle

dolphin

sea horse

seaweed

crab

coral

starfish

Space

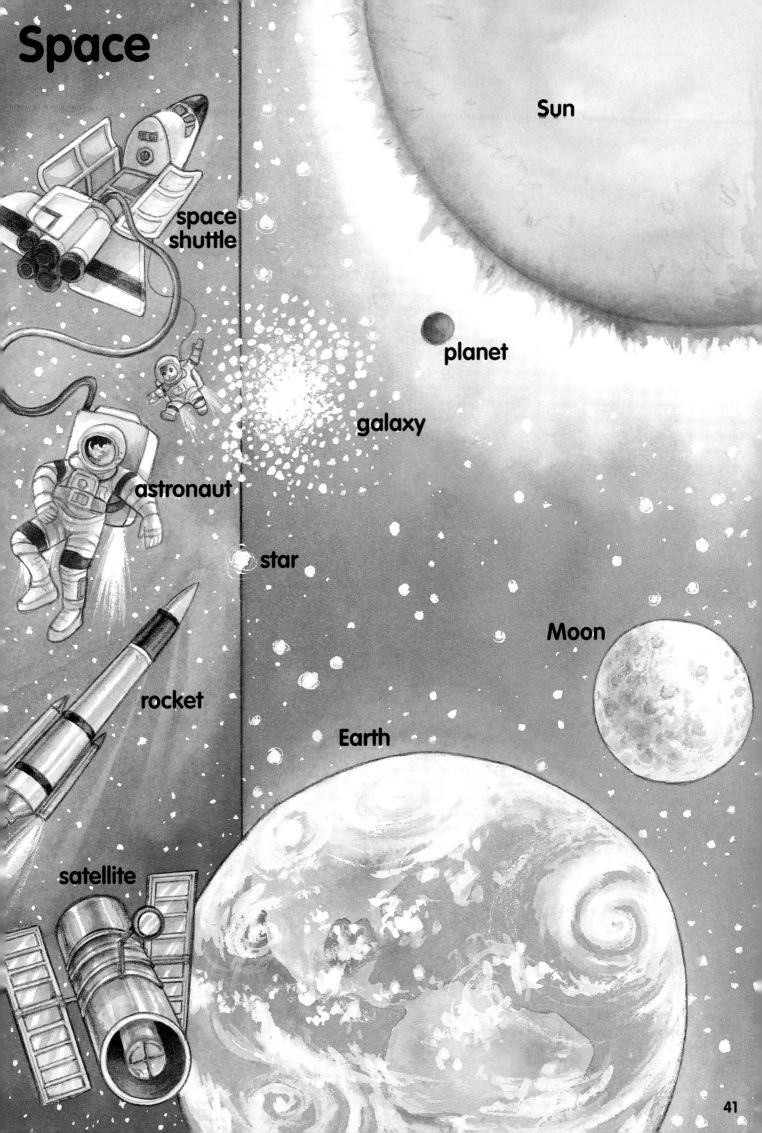

Sun

space
shuttle

planet

galaxy

astronaut

star

Moon

rocket

Earth

satellite

Seasons

snow

icicle

earmuffs

glove

snowsuit

parka

snowman

scarf

sled

mitten

boots

winter

ball

hammock

sprinkler

lemonade

sunglasses

pool

bathing suit

summer

umbrella

nest

bird

grass

raincoat

flowers

spring

rubber boots

pumpkins

backpack

costume

jacket

tree

rake

leaves

fall

43

Opposites

full

empty

dark

light

heavy

light

hot

tall

fast

cold

slow

short

alike

different

high

behind

above

low

in front of

below

44

wet

open

dry

closed

new

old

big

small

dirty

clean

off

on

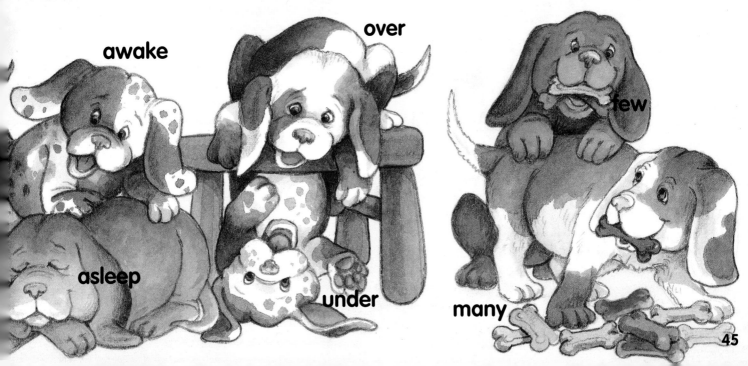

awake

over

few

asleep

under

many

45

Numbers

 **1** one

 **2** two

 **3** three

 **4** four

 **5** five

 **6** six

 **7** seven

8 eight

 **9** nine

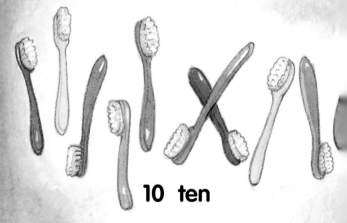 **10** ten

 **11** eleven

 **12** twelve

46

Colors

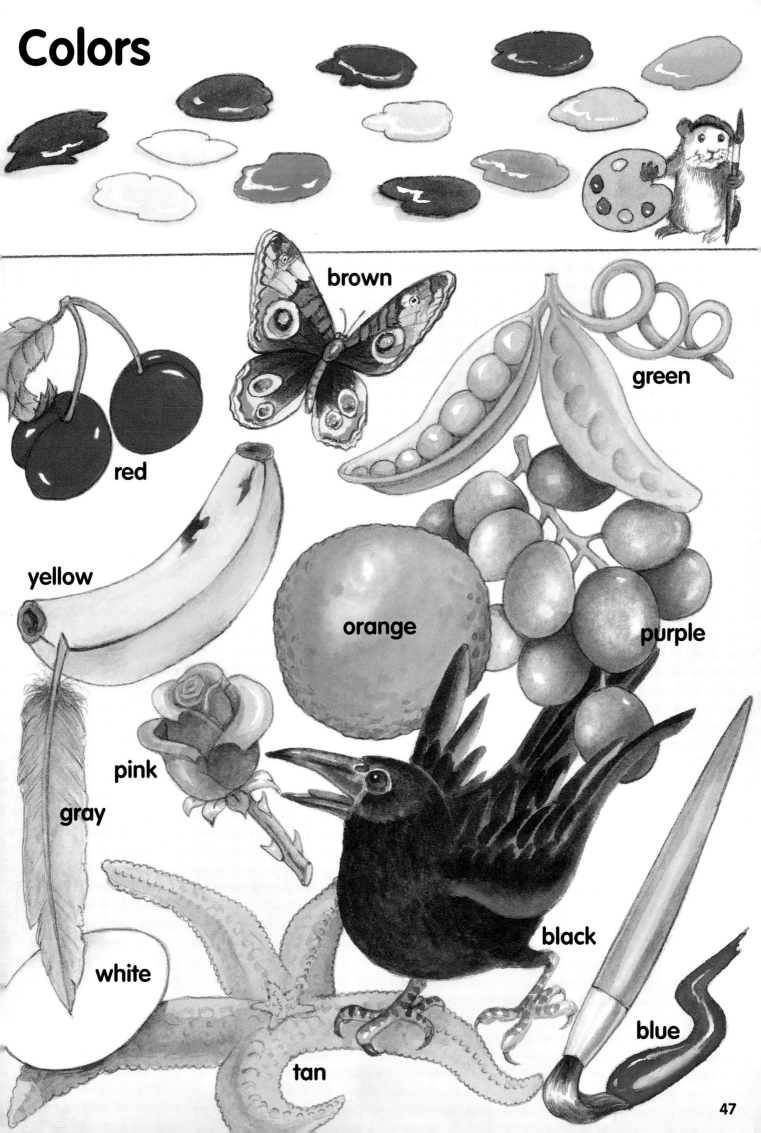

brown

green

red

yellow

orange

purple

pink

gray

white

black

blue

tan

Shapes

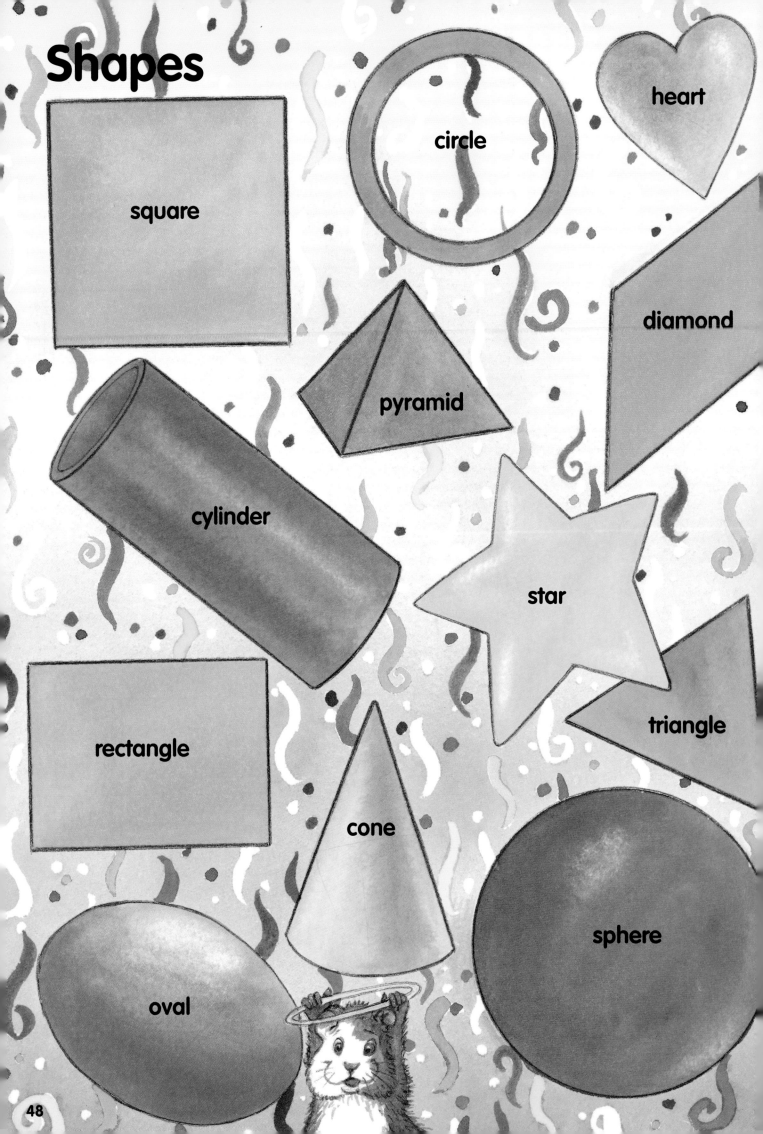

square

circle

heart

diamond

pyramid

cylinder

star

rectangle

triangle

cone

sphere

oval